HOORAY FOR SHOPPYWOOD!

Written

Illustrated

SCHOLASTIC INC.

©2014 Moose. Shopkins™ logos, names and characters are licensed
trademarks of Moose Enterprise (INT) Pty Ltd. All rights reserved.

All rights reserved. Published by Scholastic Inc., *Publishers since 1920.*
SCHOLASTIC and associated logos are trademarks and/or registered
trademarks of Scholastic Inc.

The publisher does not have any control over and does not assume any
responsibility for author or third-party websites or their content.

This book is a work of fiction. Names, characters, places, and incidents are
either the product of the author's imagination or are used fictitiously,
and any resemblance to actual persons, living or dead, business establishments,
events, or locales is entirely coincidental.

ISBN 978-1-338-12856-7

10 9 8 7 6 5 4 3 2 1   17 18 19 20 21

Printed in the U.S.A.   40

First printing 2017

Book design by Erin McMahon

CHAPTER ONE

SHOPPIES SURPRISE

"Attention, Shopville shoppers!" Popette shouted as she burst into the Small Mart. "Stop what you're doing to hear my awesome news!"

Excited whispers filled the shelves, bins, and freezers. Shopkins loved news—especially the awesome kind!

"I'm all ears!" Corny Cob declared.

"Something tells me this is going to be juicy!" Strawberry Kiss swooned.

Most curious at the Small Mart were Jessicake, Donatina, Bubbleisha, and Peppa-Mint. They were curious enough to stop doing what they loved best: shopping!

"What's the news, Popette?" Jessicake asked.

"This isn't like the time you thought you'd invented a great new popcorn flavor, is it?" Bubbleisha asked, grinning. "Choco-licorice-tunafish-chili-pepper?"

Popette wrinkled her nose. As a popcorn expert, she taste-tested every flavor ever popped in Shopville—but that flavor was one of her more *unusual* creations.

"That was not the best idea," Popette admitted. "But this is way better. You'll never guess!"

"Ooh, I know, I know!" Donatina piped up. "You watched the same movie ten times!"

Popette loved movies just as much as she loved popcorn. But she shook her head and said, "That's not my news, either."

Meanwhile, the Shopkins were getting impatient.

"What is it, Popette?" Spilt Milk called out. "Come on. Spill!"

"Yeah!" Suzie Sundae said. "Like, give us the scoop already!"

Popette couldn't wait to share any longer. She jumped up and down like a kernel in a hot-air popper and said, "Okay, okay! You know how movies totally rock my world, right?"

"Right!" Jessicake, Donatina, Bubbleisha, and Peppa-Mint said at the same time. Who in Shopville didn't know that?

"But seeing movies isn't enough anymore,"

Popette declared. "For the first time ever, I want to make my own movie!"

The minty-green bubble in Bubbleisha's mouth popped. The Shoppies looked at one another in surprise.

"Make your own movie?" Donatina repeated.

"You mean . . . like a big Hollywood director?" Bubbleisha gasped.

Popette nodded. "But I don't want to direct just any old movie," she explained. "I want to direct the next big popbuster!"

Popette's news traveled up and down the Fruit & Veg, Bakery, Pantry, and Health & Beauty aisles—until every Shopkin at the Small Mart knew Popette's super-cool plan.

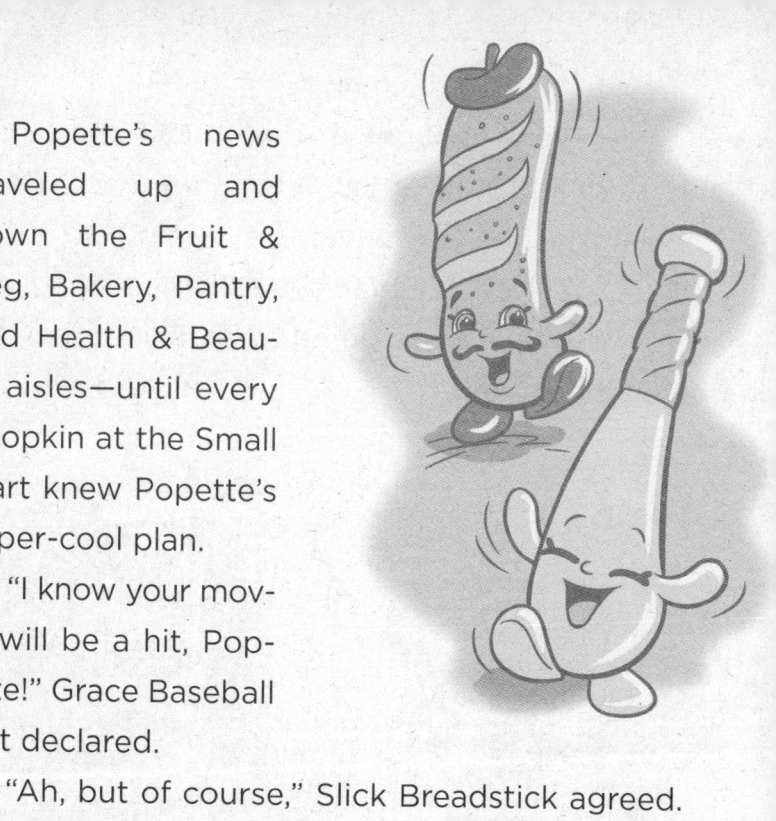

"I know your movie will be a hit, Popette!" Grace Baseball Bat declared.

"Ah, but of course," Slick Breadstick agreed. "I can smell it in zee air!"

"What will your movie be about?" Grace asked.

"The first movie I direct will be about what makes Shopville great," Popette announced. "You know, like a popumentary."

"Lots of things make Shopville great, Popette," Jessicake said. "What's the greatest of the great?"

"I haven't thought of that yet," Popette admitted. "But, no worries. When the camera starts rolling, just be yourselves."

"Ourselves?" Bubbleisha asked.

"You mean we're going to be in your movie?" Donatina asked.

"We start filming tomorrow morning at sun-up," Popette explained, "so be ready for make-up."

"Sunup?" Lippy Lips sighed from the makeup shelf. "What about my beauty sleep?"

Popette didn't seem to hear her. She was too busy thinking about what she needed to do to get ready, too.

"Okay, crew," Popette told Bowl-inda and Polly Popcorn. "I'm calling a preproduction meeting in exactly three minutes!"

"What are we waiting for?" Bowl-inda said.

"Let's get poppin'!" Polly Popcorn exclaimed.

Popette and her crew left the Small Mart for the Cinema Popcorn Cart. Over buckets of popcorn, they discussed the movie budget, equipment, and locations.

Jessicake, Donatina, Bubbleisha, and Peppa-Mint left for the Cupcake Queen Café. Over cocoa, cookies, and cupcakes, they discussed the movie, too—and how excited they were to star in it! Well, all of them except one.

"Seeing a movie being made would be cool enough," Jessicake said between licks of cupcake frosting. "But being in one is the icing on the cupcake!"

"Or the sprinkles on the donut!" Donatina added.

"I don't know," Peppa-Mint said nervously, spooning the vanilla ice cream on her berry cupcake. "I'm a little scared about being in front of the camera. What if I'm a horrible actress? But I do want to show everyone why Shopville is so great . . ."

Bubbleisha was about to tell Peppa-Mint she'd do a great job—until an unwelcome thought bubbled inside her head.

"What if . . . ," Bubbleisha asked slowly. "What if what makes Shopville great isn't great enough for an awesome movie?"

"Not great enough?" Jessicake repeated.

"What do you mean, Bubbleisha?" Donatina asked.

"I mean, what if Popette's big popbuster," Bubbleisha said in almost a whisper, "becomes a flopbuster?"

CHAPTER TWO

POPBUSTER OR FLOPBUSTER?

The Shoppies became silent as they thought about Bubbleisha's question—until they all began speaking at once.

"A flopbuster?" Donatina cried. "That would be Popette's worst nightmare!"

"There's got to be something we can do to make sure Popette's movie is a hit," Peppa-Mint insisted.

"But what?" Bubbleisha asked.

Jessicake straightened up in her chair and gave her friends a reassuring smile.

"Let's not get carried away. Why don't we shop around for ideas?" Jessicake suggested. "If there's anything we know how to do, it's shop! Right?"

"Right!" Donatina, Bubbleisha, and Peppa-Mint replied with high fives all around.

The Shoppies finished their treats. After saying good-bye, they went their separate ways to brainstorm ideas for Popette's movie.

"There are lots of different kinds of movies," Bubbleisha wondered out loud, "but what kind would be a sure hit for Popette and Shopville?"

Tapping her chin thoughtfully, Bubbleisha said, "How about a candy scavenger hunt . . . followed by a demonstration on how to get gooey bubble gum off the soles of your shoes?"

Bubbleisha raised an eyebrow at Gumball Gabby and Bubblicious to see what they thought.

"Um . . . that's a nice idea, Bubbleisha," Gumball Gabby said politely.

"It's not the most exciting, though," Bubblicious added. "It doesn't really scream 'Shopville!'"

Bubbleisha's shoulders drooped. "You're right. What should I do?" she asked. "Coming up with ideas is harder than I thought!"

"Why don't you chew on it awhile, Bubbleisha?"

14

Bubblicious suggested gently.

"Good idea," Gumball Gabby agreed. "As they say, you're always on the ball—a big, juicy gumball!" She giggled.

Candy always did make Bubbleisha think better. She popped a purple gumball into her mouth and began to chew.

As she tried to think of new ideas, Bubbleisha blew a bubble . . . a big bubble . . . an even bigger and bigger bubble—until it lifted her a few inches off the ground!

"Wow!" Bubblicious exclaimed after the bubble popped and Bubbleisha landed gently on the ground. "That was the most ginormous bubble I ever saw!"

"Me too," Gabby said. "And we know bubbles!"

Bubbleisha knew bubbles, too. And at that moment, she suddenly knew something else.

"That ginormous bubble," Bubbleisha declared, "just gave me a ginormous idea!"

*　　*　　*　　*　　*

Meanwhile, at Donatina's Donut Delights, Donatina came up with ideas, too—a whole lot of not-so-great ideas.

"How about a science fiction film about life on Planet Cronut?" Donatina said dreamily, staring out the window.

Daisy Donut and Rolly Donut's eyes glazed over.

"Too out there?" Donatina asked, seeing their faces.

"Just a bit," Daisy said carefully.

"But you'll think of something, Donatina," Rolly Donut insisted. "You're already on a roll."

"Like this!" a voice shouted out.

"Who said that?" Donatina asked.

Turning toward the shelves, Donatina gasped. D'Lish Donut and Dolly Donut were leaping off the shelves, rolling and flipping over each other with the skill of circus acrobats!

"Ta-daaa!" D'Lish Donut sang when they were done, striking a pose. "What do you think?"

"I think," Donatina said slowly, "that you just gave me an idea!"

* * * * *

Over at the Cool Dream Ice Cream Parlor, Peppa-Mint had no ideas. She was having a major brain freeze!

"What am I supposed to do in this movie? I'm

not getting any-thing!" Peppa-Mint groaned. "Except maybe another big meltdowwwwwn!"

Oh no! Carla Cone and Icy-Bowl had seen Peppa-Mint's meltdowns before, and they weren't pretty.

"Keep thinking, Peppa-Mint," Icy-Bowl told her. "We can come up with something!"

"Yes, Peppa-Mint," Carla agreed. "You'll solve the mystery for sure."

Mystery? Peppa-Mint glanced up with a smile. Did Carla just say *mystery*?

"Icy, Carla, guess what?" Peppa-Mint said happily. "I know the perfect solution!"

If only Jessicake was so lucky.

"Maybe Popette can make a movie about baking cupcakes," Jessicake said as she strolled through Shopville with Coco Cupcake and Cherry Cake. "But what if Popette's audience doesn't like cupcakes?"

Jessicake stopped walking to heave a sigh. "Why is coming up with ideas harder than frosting left out on the counter all day?"

Uh-oh. When Jessicake was worried, Coco Cupcake and Cherry Cake were worried, too!

"We have to do something to make Jessicake feel better," Coco whispered to Cherry. "But what do we say?"

"Why say it," Cherry whispered back, "when we can sing it instead?"

Coco and Cherry hopped in front of Jessicake. After a few fancy dance steps, they began to sing:

"Cupcakes, cupcakes, so sweet and creamy! Did we happen to mention that we're also dreamy?"

Jessicake smiled through Coco and Cherry's whole number. After they each took a bow, she clapped her hands and cheered.

"That number takes the cake!" Jessicake exclaimed. "Why didn't I think of that?"

"You just needed a little help," Coco Cupcake answered with a smile. "Now let's surprise Popette tomorrow with the old razzle-dazzle!"

* * * * *

Jessicake spent the rest of the day working on plans for the movie with Coco Cupcake and Cherry Cake. They couldn't wait to star in a popumentary.

Would Popette like her idea? And Donatina's, Bubbleisha's, and Peppa-Mint's ideas, too? There was only one way to find out: lights, camera, action!

CHAPTER THREE

ICE SCREAM

"Camera?" Popette asked, looking up from her list of movie equipment.

"Check!" Bowl-inda said, smiling as she lifted the all-important movie camera.

"Lights?" Popette asked next.

"Check!" Polly Popcorn said, shining the bright movie light in Popette's face.

Popette blinked, then asked, "Makeup?"

"Check!" Lippy Lips replied while checking out her own reflection in Mindy Mirror.

It was the morning of the movie shoot. Popette Productions had the lights. It had the camera. Now was the time for the most

awesome part of making a movie: Action!

"Good job, crew," Popette praised. "Now, let's show the world what makes Shopville great. Let's make a movie!"

The Shopkins crew cheered. So far Popette was an awesome director. She even looked just like a director in her popcorn-yellow *Popette Productions* cap!

"On to our first location," Popette stated. "The Cool Dream Ice Cream Parlor."

But when Popette and the others entered the Cool Dream Ice Cream Parlor, they thought they were in the wrong place.

The usual cheery café tables and chairs were gone. In their place was plain old-timey furniture. On the walls were fancy, old-fashioned portraits of Carla Cone and Icy-Bowl. And in the middle of the room, there was a giant ice cream sundae with just-as-giant toppings!

"Am I dreaming?" Popette asked slowly as she gazed around the weird room. "This place is a total mystery!"

"Precisely!" a voice declared.

Before Popette could ask who said that, Peppa-Mint stepped out from behind the giant sundae. Just like the ice cream parlor, she looked different, too. Instead of her usual ice-cream-colored clothes, she wore a bulky tweed coat and matching cap.

"Um . . . hi, Peppa-Mint?" Popette asked, still confused. "What's poppin'?"

"Ah! You may know me as Peppa-Mint," Peppa-Mint replied with a fancy accent. "But today, I am Detective Sherlock Cones, here to solve the mystery of the missing cherry."

Bowl-inda looked at the top of the sundae. "What cherry?" she asked.

"Precisely!" Peppa-Mint shouted again, causing Popette and her friends to jump back in surprise. "Early this morning, a cherry disappeared from the top of this banana rocky-road ice cream sundae. A cold case, indeed."

"It can't be that cold," Polly said.

"What do you mean?" Peppa-Mint asked, examining Polly's face through her magnifying glass.

Bowl-inda pointed to the sundae. "Because," she said, "that supersized ice cream sundae is melting!"

"Melting?" Peppa-Mint gulped.

She looked up and—*SPLAT*—a huge drop of ice cream landed on her head, followed by a landslide of melty ice cream, tumbling giant marshmallows, nuts, sprinkles, and chocolate chips!

"Look out below!" Carla Cone shouted.

"It's an avalanche!" Icy-Bowl exclaimed. "An ice cream avalanche!"

Peppa-Mint, Popette, and the Shopkins ran for cover as the ice cream came gushing toward them!

CHAPTER FOUR

BROADWAY OOz-ICAL

The ice cream flood finally stopped. So did the tumble of toppings.

"Wow," Peppa-Mint said, staring at the mess. "And they say I have meltdowns."

Meanwhile, the director was having a meltdown of her own.

"Cut, cut, cut!" Popette shouted. "This isn't the movie scene I had in mind!"

"Sorry, Popette," said Peppa-Mint quietly. "I thought a mystery story

would make a great movie."

Popette heaved a big sigh. She knew Peppa-Mint was just trying to help.

"Thanks, Peppa-Mint," Popette said. "But a mystery isn't what makes Shopville great."

"But we did find the missing cherry!" Icy-Bowl said, pointing to a big red cherry in the middle of a puddle. "How great is that?"

To help Peppa-Mint clean the melty mess, Popette called Molly Mops and her friends.

"Don't worry, Peppa-Mint!" Molly Mops said cheerily. "I've got a handle on this."

The film crew left the ice cream parlor for their next movie location: the Cupcake Queen Café!

"The next scene should be a piece of cake," Popette said hopefully. "What could go wrong

30

with Jessicake? She's always calm, cool, and collected—she'll be great in front of the camera."

But when Popette opened the door to the café, something seemed strange. Instead of looking like the Cupcake Queen Café, the place looked like a Broadway musical stage!

"What now?" Popette cried.

Glowing under a spotlight in the middle of the room stood an enormous cupcake with swirly pink frosting. On each side of the cupcake stood a towering soda bottle.

"Anybody home?" Popette called.

A blast of music made everyone jump. Then

Coco Cupcake and Cherry Cake peeked out from behind the cupcake. The Shopkins wore glittery top hats and big smiles as they began to sing:

"When life throws you heartache, just reach for a cupcake!"

The top of the giant cupcake flew open. A sparkly-suited Jessicake popped up from inside, singing: "Iron out life's wrinkles—with frosting and some sprinkles!"

Still singing, Jessicake climbed down from the cupcake just as both soda bottle caps burst off. Popette and her crew ooh'd and aah'd as colorful soda gushed up from the bottles with a loud *WHOOSH*!

"What could be sweeter," Jessicake kept singing, "on the cupcake sweet-o-meter?"

Jessicake's Broadway show was not what Popette was expecting, but it was pretty pop-tacular. Maybe this was exactly what her movie needed! Everything looked amazing—until the colorful soda fountains suddenly switched directions. Before Jessicake knew what was happening, they were spewing super-sticky soda all over the café!

CHAPTER FIVE

BUBBLE TROUBLE

"Put a lid on it!" Jessicake cried as both bottles spurted out of control. "Two lids!"

Coco and Cherry scurried up the soda bottles to replace the lids. The gushing stopped. Popette and her crew had covered their movie equipment just in time. But everything else in the Cupcake Queen Café was a dripping mess—including Popette!

"Cut! Cut!" Popette shouted as Bowl-inda and Polly turned off the camera and lights.

"Sorry, Popette," Jessicake said. "I thought a lighthearted Broadway musical would be perfect for your popbuster."

"Thanks, Jessicake," Popette said with a small smile. "But my popbuster just became a slop-buster."

"And I was so ready for my close-up," Coco Cupcake said sadly.

"Now we're ready for your tidy-up!" Molly Mops announced as she and her crew marched into the café, ready to clean up yet another movie disaster.

Dejected but still determined, Popette Productions packed up and headed to the next location, the Dandy Candy Store.

"We have to make up for lost time, crew," Popette told them on the way.

"Did you say makeup?" Lippy Lips asked excitedly.

"That's us!" Mindy Mirror declared.

Popette's shoulders drooped. She wished she felt as excited as her crew, but all she felt was worry. What if the next scene turned sour, too?

When they reached the Dandy Candy Store, Popette saw Bubbleisha standing outside.

"Good morning, Ms. Director!" Bubbleisha said with a smile.

Popette smiled, too—with relief. So far, there was nothing weird about the Dandy Candy Store or Bubbleisha.

"Good morning, Bubbleisha," Popette said.

While Lippy Lips and Mindy Mirror worked to give Bubbleisha a look sure to pop on camera, Popette described the first scene:

"Okay, Bubbleisha. You just stepped out of the candy store with the juiciest-looking gumball you ever saw. You pop it into your mouth and begin to chew!"

Bubbleisha tossed an orange gumball into her mouth. "Like this?" she asked between chews.

"Perfect!" Popette exclaimed. "Now just put your lips together and blow a bubble!"

Bubbleisha did blow a bubble. She kept blowing until the bubble grew bigger and bigger and bigger, lifting her, Gumball Gabby, and Bubblicious several feet into the air!

As Bubbleisha rose higher and higher, Popette knew something was wrong. At the rate they were going, they'd soon be in outer space!

"Bubbleisha! Gabby! Bubblicious!" Popette called up to her flyaway friends. "Come down!"

CHAPTER SIX

NO BUSINESS LIKE DOUGH BUSINESS

"We can't come down, Popette!" Gumball Gabby shouted down.

"This bubble ain't bursting," Bubblicious added.

Popette shouted for help. Suddenly, the door of the Dandy Candy Store flew open, and an army of candy Shopkins raced out.

"*Quelle catastrophique!*" Macca Roon gasped when she saw Bubbleisha.

"I wish there was something we could do!" Cheeky Chocolate wailed.

The candy brigade sprung into action. Cheeky Chocolate and Le'Quorice jumped into a

seesaw formation. Then Minnie Mintie catapulted off Cheeky toward the flyaway bubble until—
BOOM—she hit the bubble, bursting it in midair!

As Bubbleisha and the Shopkins began to fall, Jiggly Jelly raced underneath to the rescue. The other candy Shopkins cheered as their flying friends landed on Jiggly Jelly one at a time and bounced gently off her onto the ground.

"Don't you just love when sticky situations have sweet endings?" Lolli Poppins sighed.

"Bittersweet," Cheeky Chocolate said when she saw Popette's frown. "I think the director is about to blow up next."

"Cut! Cut!" Popette shouted. "Cut!"

"I'm sorry, Popette." Bubbleisha shrugged. "I thought you'd like a little action and adventure in your movie."

"Too bad it turned into a misadventure," Popette said. "But thanks for trying, anyway."

Popette turned to her crew. "Let's blow this popcorn stand," she said, "and head to our next location."

On the way, Bowl-inda and Polly watched as their director began looking sadder and sadder.

"Don't worry, Popette," Bowl-inda said.

"We know your big popbuster is just one scene away!" Polly Popcorn exclaimed.

"Yes, don't give up now, darling," Lippy Lips said. "There's still time to make this movie fabulous!"

Popette smiled. Her friends did make her feel better. And dollars to donuts, her next scene at the donut shop would be a sweet success!

As they entered Donatina's Donut Delights, Popette felt even more hopeful. Everything inside looked just like it always did: bright, cheerful, and full of donuts.

"Scene one, take one!" Popette shouted after all equipment was in place. "Quiet on the set . . . and we are ready to roll!"

" . . . Did someone say roll?" a voice asked.

Popette would recognize that voice anywhere.

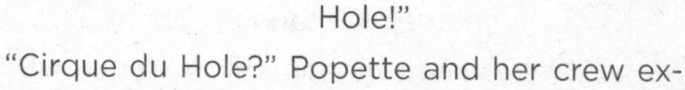

"Donatina?" she called out. "Is that you?"

Donatina stepped out from behind the counter wearing a red-and-black suit, boots, and a top hat like a circus ringmaster!

"Ladies and gentlemen and Shopkins of all ages!" Donatina shouted out. "Please give a *hole* lot of love to the magnificent . . . amazing . . . a-glazing Cirque du Hole!"

"Cirque du Hole?" Popette and her crew exclaimed.

The sound of a drumroll filled the air as Shopkins jumped off the shelves. D'Lish Donut grabbed on to hanging lamps, swinging like a circus acrobat. A group of frosted donuts formed a pyramid while Daisy Donut and Rolly Donut rolled and flipped into the air.

"Holey cow!" Popette cried as they watched the surprise show.

"And nooooow," Donatina said, waving a white-gloved hand at a huge vat on the counter, "please give it up for the incredible Dolly Donut!"

Donatina blew into a whistle and Dolly Donut appeared, doing a series of impressive flips and cartwheels before leaping into the vat. Then Dolly leapt back out, sparkling with powdered sugar! She wagged her tail and took a bow.

"Is this the greatest dough on earth," Donatina declared, "or what?"

Dolly Donut continued to perform her tricks. She somersaulted up the counter straight toward the vat. But before she could jump into it, she slammed into the vat with a huge *BAM*!

Donatina and the Shopkins gasped as the huge vat of powdered sugar began to tip—right toward Popette and her crew!

CHAPTER SEVEN

STOP THE POP

"Noooo!" Popette shouted as powdered sugar rained on her and her crew.

"Sorry!" Daisy Donut shouted after the shower of sugar finally stopped. "Dolly likes to go out with a bang—literally!"

"I'm sorry, too, Popette," Donatina said as she took off her ringmaster's hat, shaking the sugar off the brim. "I thought you'd want a circus scene in your popbuster movie."

Popette turned and headed toward the door, leaving a trail of powdered-sugar footprints behind her.

"Thanks, Donatina," Popette said, "but making a movie doesn't matter anymore."

"Why not?" Donatina asked.

Upon reaching the door, Popette replied, "Because I quit!"

"Quit?" Donatina and the Shopkins gasped in unison.

"I don't want to make movies anymore," Popette explained. "All I want to do is watch movies and eat popcorn. Tons and tons of popcorn!"

Popette stormed out of the shop, letting the door slam behind her.

"Um . . . is that a wrap?" Bowl-inda asked.

For Popette, it was. In no time she was inside the Cinema Popcorn Cart, popping buckets of popcorn. Buckets and buckets and buckets of popcorn in all flavors!

"Caramel crunch, nutty chocolate, cheddar cheesy," Popette said as she shoveled more and more popped kernels into her mouth. "Spicy barbecue, salt and vinegar, tropical mango—"

"Popette," Bowl-inda said gently, "I think you've had enough."

"Enough of making movies!" Popette declared. "As for popcorn—one can never have enough of that."

As quick as the pop of a kernel, word about

Popette spread through Shopville. Soon, more and more Shopkins were gathering inside the Cinema Popcorn Cart to see how they could help.

"Don't give up making movies, Popette," June Balloon said cheerfully.

"We know you can nail it!" Polly Polish insisted.

"Yes, of course," agreed Slick Breadstick. "And I had hoped I would be chosen as zee leading man in your next film!"

"Thanks, guys," Popette said kindly. "But it's no use buttering me up."

She looked around, a wild look in her eyes. "Butter . . . where's the extra buttered bucket? Where?"

The Shopkins stepped back helplessly. Wasn't there anything they could do to stop Popette's popcorn meltdown?

"What was I thinking?" Popcorn wailed to herself as more and more popcorn piled at her feet. "I can't direct a movie . . . I can't even direct traffic!"

Popped kernels in dozens of flavors, savory and sweet, piled higher and higher—until Popette was buried up to her neck in popcorn!

"What have I done?" Popette cried.

The Shopkins raced over to the mountain of popcorn and Popette.

"Don't worry, Popette," Polly Popcorn cried. "We'll get you out!"

Polly and Bowl-inda scampered up the mountain of popcorn to reach Popette, only to slide down the slippery butter and caramel to the floor!

"Maybe you can eat your way out, Popette!" Bowl-inda suggested.

"Eat?" Popette groaned, her face turning green. "Not another kernel—please!"

"Or . . . maybe not," Bowl-inda quickly said.

The Shopkins saw that Popette was in trouble. They also knew that they had to help. But how?

"I thought every-one's movie scenes were over-the-top," Popette said sadly. "But look at me! I'm even more over-the-

top than Donatina, Jessicake, Peppa-Mint, or Bubbleisha."

Donatina? Jessicake? Peppa-Mint? Bubbleisha? The names of Popette's Shoppie friends gave the Shopkins an idea!

"Don't go anywhere, Popette!" June Balloon called back as a brigade of Shopkins raced toward the door. "We'll be right back!"

CHAPTER EIGHT

SHOPKINS TO THE RESCUE!

Help was not hard to find. That's because Donatina, Jessicake, Peppa-Mint, and Bubble-isha were still cleaning up each of their mega-movie messes.

"Attention, Shopville!" June Balloon shouted as she floated by the Cool Dream Ice Cream Parlor. "Popette is in trouble and needs our help!"

"Help?" Peppa-Mint gasped. "I'm there!"

At the same time, Toasty Pop ran straight to the Cupcake Queen Café and opened the door.

"Popette is toast. I repeat, Popette is toast!" Toasty shouted into the shop. "Not that there's anything wrong with that, but—"

"—I get it, Toasty," Jessicake cut in, wiping frosting off her hands. "Popette needs my help and I'm on the way!"

Meanwhile, Donatina was getting a visit from Tammy TV.

"News flash, news flash," Tammy announced. "Sources tell us Poperation Rescue is underway!"

"Poperation Rescue, hmm?" Donatina said. "If that means Popette needs help, sign me up."

Last but not least, a determined Milk Bud scampered into the Dandy Candy Store. His tail wagged fast and furiously as he began to bark:

"Woof, woof, woof, woof, woof, woof, WOOF!"

"You say Popette popped herself up to her neck in kernels and she can't get out?" Bubbleisha gasped. "Thanks, Milk Bud. I'm right behind you."

Using both arms, Bubbleisha grabbed a super-sized peppermint stick on display in the store. "But first," she said with a grin, "I think I know exactly how to get her out."

At the exact same minute, Peppa-Mint, Donatina, Jessicake, and Bubbleisha stormed the Cinema Popcorn Cart, the giant peppermint stick in tow.

"Grab this!" Bubbleisha said as they held the peppermint stick out to Popette, "and we'll pull you out!"

Popette stared at the peppermint stick and asked, "Is it strong enough?"

"Don't worry," Bubbleisha replied. "It's in mint condition!"

After Popette got a good grip, Jessicake told the others, "On the count of three, everybody pull. One . . . two . . ."

"Pull!" the girls yelled as they tugged the giant candy cane with all their might. Slowly but gently, Popette popped out of the popcorn pyramid with only a few kernels spilling to the ground.

"Well done!" Toasty Pop shouted.

"I'm so happy, I could cry!" Spilt Milk sniffed.

A round of hearty cheers filled the Cinema Popcorn Cart. Poperation Rescue was a huge success, and Popette was safe. But nobody was happier than Popette!

"Thanks for saving me," Popette told Mint, Donatina, Jessicake, and Bubbleish for trying to save my movie, too."

"No problem," Peppa-Mint said happily.

"That's what friends are for," Jessicake added.

"Exactly!" Popette said, waving her arms in

...he air. "You guys, I just realized something super important!"

"Um . . . that you have tons of leftover popcorn?" Bubbleisha asked.

Popette shook her head.

"I finally realized what makes Shopville great," Popette said with a big smile. "And it's all the amazing friends you can find here!"

Everyone cheered once again as Popette, Jessicake, Donatina, Bubbleisha, and Peppa-Mint shared a group hug.

"And I got the whole thing on film!" Bowlinda said, lifting the camera.

"That's a wrap!" Polly Popcorn declared with a grin. "At last!"

But for all five Shoppie friends—the fun was just beginning!

* * * * *

"Look at the crowds!" Donatina gasped.

"Sweet!" Bubbleisha exclaimed.

It was the week after Poperation Rescue. It

was also opening night for Popette's [...] buster movie.

Popette, Peppa-Mint, Donatina, Jes[...] and Bubbleisha stood on the red fruity-roll-up carpet, dressed in their most glam outfits. As they watched Shopkins file into the movie theater, they couldn't believe their eyes!

"Everybody wants to see *Popped Till She Dropped!*" Peppa-Mint said, pointing at the sign, "directed by Shopville's most famous movie director: Popette!"

"Even the Pop-arazzi is here!" Popette said excitedly, fluffing her curls and waving to the cameras.

"You bet we are, Popette!" Cam Camera shouted. "Now say 'cheese flavored!'"

As the cameras flashed, Jessicake asked, "So Popette, do you still want to change Shopville to Shoppywood?"

Popette shook her head as she smiled at her four best friends.

"You know I don't like to be corny," Popette said. "But I like Shopville just the way it is!"

create a
dream
menu with
Jessicake!

Plan a
game night
party with
Donatina!

Write your own
movie scene
with Popette

AND MUCH
MORE!

GET YOUR CREATIVITY ON WITH YOUR VERY
OWN FUN-TASTIC FILL-IN JOURNAL!